The Beginning of the ARMADILLOES

For Robert

Find out more about
Rudyard Kipling's
JUST so STORIES
at Shoo Rayner's fabulous website,
www.shoo-rayner.co.uk

First published in 2007 by Orchard Books
First paperback publication in 2008

ORCHARD BOOKS
338 Euston Road, London NW1 3BH
Orchard Books Australia
Level 17/207 Kent St, Sydney, NSW 2000

ISBN 978 1 84616 403 3 (hardback)
ISBN 978 1 84616 411 8 (paperback)

Retelling and illustrations © Shoo Rayner 2007

A CIP catalogue record for this book is available from the British Library.

1 3 5 7 9 10 8 6 4 2 (hardback)
1 3 5 7 9 10 8 6 4 2 (paperback)

Printed and bound in England by Antony Rowe Ltd, Chippenham, Wiltshire

Orchard Books is a division of Hachette Children's Books,
an Hachette Livre UK company.

www.orchardbooks.co.uk

Rudyard Kipling's
JUST SO STORIES

The Beginning of the
ARMADILLOES

Retold and illustrated by
SHOO RAYNER

ORCHARD BOOKS

Long, long ago, at the very beginning of time, when everything was just getting sorted out, Stickly-Prickly Hedgehog lived on the banks of the turbid Amazon, eating shelly snails and things.

He had a friend,
Slow-and-Solid
Tortoise, who ate
mostly green lettuces.

There was also a Painted Jaguar living on the banks of the turbid Amazon. He ate everything that he could catch. When he could not catch deer or monkeys he caught frogs and beetles.

When he could not catch frogs and beetles he went to his Mother Jaguar, who told him how to eat Hedgehogs and Tortoises.

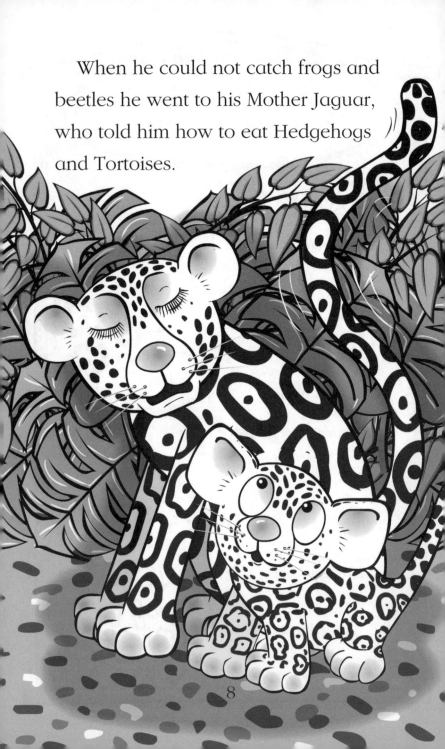

"My son," she said, "when you find a Hedgehog you must drop him into the water, then he will uncoil."

"When you catch a Tortoise you must scoop him out of his shell with your paw."

One beautiful night, on the banks of the turbid Amazon, Painted Jaguar found Stickly-Prickly Hedgehog and Slow-and-Solid Tortoise sitting behind a clump of bushes.

Stickly-Prickly curled himself up into a ball, because he was a Hedgehog.

Slow-and-Solid pulled his head and feet into his shell, because he was a Tortoise.

"Now listen to me," said Painted
Jaguar, "because this is very important.
My mother said that when I meet
a Hedgehog I have to drop him into
the water and then he will uncoil.

"And when I meet a Tortoise I am to scoop him out of his shell with my paw. So, which of you is Hedgehog and which is Tortoise? Because, to save my spots, I can't tell."

"Are you sure about what your mother said?" said Stickly-Prickly. "Are you quite sure? Perhaps she said that when you uncoil a Tortoise you must shell him out of the water with a scoop?"

"I don't think it was that," said Painted Jaguar, feeling a little puzzled. "Say it again slowly."

"Perhaps your mother said that when you water a Hedgehog you must drop him into your paw," said Slow-and-Solid.

"You're making my spots ache," said Painted Jaguar, "and besides, I didn't ask you for advice. I only want to know which of you is Hedgehog and which is Tortoise."

"I shan't tell you," said Stickly-Prickly, "but you can scoop me out of my shell if you like."

"Aha!" said Painted Jaguar. "Now I know you're Tortoise."

Painted Jaguar darted out his
paddy-paw just as Stickly-Prickly
curled himself up, and of course
Jaguar's paddy-paw was filled
with prickles.

Worse than that, he
knocked Stickly-Prickly
away and away into
the bushes.

Painted Jaguar put his paddy-paw into his mouth, and of course the prickles hurt him worse than ever. As soon as he could speak he said, "If he isn't Tortoise, then who are you?"

"I am Tortoise," said Slow-and-Solid. "Your mother was quite right. She said that you were to scoop me out of my shell with your paw."

"You didn't say she said that a minute ago," said Painted Jaguar, sucking his paddy-paw.

"Well, suppose you say that I said that she said something quite different," said Tortoise. "It doesn't matter, because if she said what you said I said she said, it's just the same as if I said what she said she said. So, if you want to see me swim away you should drop me into the water."

"I don't believe you," said Painted Jaguar. "I don't think you want to be dropped in the water at all. Go on, then! Jump in, and be quick about it."

Before Jaguar could change his mind, Slow-and-Solid quietly dived into the turbid Amazon, swam underwater for a long way, and came out on the bank where Stickly-Prickly was waiting for him.

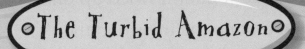

The Turbid Amazon

The Turbid Amazon is quite like soup – a living soup. In the thick brown water that flows lazily down to the sea, you will find millions of:

eels

piranhas

leeches

snails

water beetles

weeds

nameless disgusting things

Painted Jaguar howled up and down among the trees and the bushes by the side of the turbid Amazon, till his mother came.

"Son, son!" said his mother, graciously waving her tail, "what have you been doing that you shouldn't have done?"

Graciously Waving Tails

If you've got a tail, use it!

Flick it at the end.

Ripple it down the middle.

Curl it slowly and languorously.

"I scooped something out of its shell, and my paw is full of per-ickles," said Painted Jaguar.

"Son, son!" said his mother, "that was a Hedgehog. You should drop hedgehogs into the water."

"I did that to the other thing. He said he was a Tortoise, and I didn't believe him. Let's go and live somewhere else. They are too clever on the turbid Amazon for poor me!"

"Son, son!" said his mother, "listen and remember. A Hedgehog curls up into a ball and his prickles stick out every which way at once."

"A Tortoise can't curl himself up,"
Mother Jaguar went on, still graciously
waving her tail. "He can only pull his
head and legs into his shell."

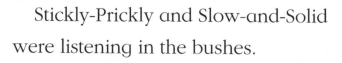

Stickly-Prickly and Slow-and-Solid were listening in the bushes.

"I don't like Mother Jaguar one little bit," whispered Stickly-Prickly. "Even Painted Jaguar can't forget those directions. It's a pity I can't swim."

"And it's a pity
I can't curl up," said
Slow-and-Solid."

Painted Jaguar sat on the banks of the turbid Amazon sucking prickles out of his paws and saying to himself:

"Can't curl, but can swim,
Slow-Solid, that's him!
Curls up, but can't swim,
Stickly-Prickly, that's him!"

"He'll never forget that in a month of Sundays," said Stickly-Prickly. "Hold up my chin, Slow-and-Solid. I'm going to learn to swim."

"Excellent!" said Slow-and-Solid, holding up Stickly-Prickly's chin, while he splashed in the waters of the turbid Amazon. "You'll make a fine swimmer yet," he said. "Now, if you can unlace my back-plates a little, I'll see if I can do some curling up."

Stickly-Prickly unlaced Tortoise's back-plates, so that by twisting and straining, Slow-and-Solid actually managed to curl up a bit.

Then Stickly-Prickly practiced swimming side-stroke, and Slow-and-Solid unlaced more of his plates and did some bending.

Swimming and Bending

When swimming it is best to hold your breath and not breathe in. You can breathe out in small bubbles.

When bending it is better to breathe out – in one great puff!

"Don't grunt quite so much,"
said Stickly-Prickly, "or Painted
Jaguar might hear us."

Then Stickly-Prickly dived under water, and practiced holding his breath, and Slow-and-Solid practiced putting his hind legs behind his ears.

"Excellent!" said Stickly-Prickly. "But your back-plates are all overlapping now, instead of lying side by side."

"Well," said Slow-and-Solid, "your prickles have melted into one another, and you're growing to look a bit like a pinecone."

"Am I?" said Stickly-Prickly.
"That comes from soaking in
the water. Oh, won't Painted
Jaguar be surprised!"

The next day, Stickly-Prickly
and Tortoise looked so different,
they were almost the same.

Painted Jaguar was astonished when he saw them. He fell backwards three times without stopping, over his own painted tail.

"Good morning!" said Stickly-Prickly. "And how is your dear, gracious mummy today?"

"She is quite well, thank you," said Painted Jaguar; "but you must forgive me if I don't recall your names."

"Don't you remember what your mother told you?" said Stickly-Prickly.

"Can't curl, but can swim,
Slow-Solid, that's him!
Curls up, but can't swim,
Stickly-Prickly, that's him!"

Then they both curled themselves up and rolled round and round Painted Jaguar till his eyes turned cartwheels in his head.

He ran wailing to his mother. "Mother," he said, "there are two new animals in the woods today, and the one that you said couldn't swim, swims, and the one that you said couldn't curl up, curls. They've gone shares in their prickles, because both of them are scaly all over!"

"Son, son!" said Mother Jaguar, graciously waving her tail, "a Hedgehog is a Hedgehog, and a Tortoise is a Tortoise. They can never be anything else."

"But it isn't a Hedgehog, and it isn't a Tortoise. It's a little bit of both, and I don't know its proper name."

"Nonsense!" said Mother Jaguar. "Everything has its proper name. I should call it 'Armadillo', and leave it well alone."

45

So Painted Jaguar did just as he was told. And from that day to this, no one on the banks of the turbid Amazon has ever called Stickly-Prickly or Slow-and-Solid anything except Armadillo.

There are Hedgehogs and Tortoises in other places, of course, but the real, old and clever kind, with their scales lying lippety-lappety like pine-cones, that live on the banks of the turbid Amazon, are still called Armadilloes, because they are so clever.

Rudyard Kipling's
JUST SO STORIES

Retold and illustrated by
SHOO RAYNER

All priced at £8.99

Rudyard Kipling's Just So Stories are available from all good bookshops,
or can be ordered direct from
the publisher: Orchard Books, PO BOX 29, Douglas IM99 1BQ
Credit card orders please telephone 01624 836000
or fax 01624 837033 or visit our internet site: www.orchardbooks.co.uk
or e-mail: bookshop@enterprise.net for details.

To order please quote title, author and ISBN
and your full name and address.
Cheques and postal orders should be made payable to 'Bookpost plc.'
Postage and packing is FREE within the UK
(overseas customers should add £2.00 per book).

Prices and availability are subject to change.